# HALLOWEEN HULLA-BOO-LU

BuzzPop

# BuzzPop

An imprint of Little Bee Books, Inc.
251 Park Avenue South, New York, NY 10010

BuzzPop is a trademark of Little Bee Books, Inc.,
and associated colophon is a trademark of Little Bee Books, Inc.

Manufactured in China HOX 0719

First Edition 1 3 5 7 9 10 8 6 4 2
ISBN 978-1-4998-0876-6

buzzpopbooks.com

Under license by:
©2019 Moose Enterprise (INT) Pty Ltd. Shoppies™ logos, names,
and characters are licensed trademarks of Moose Enterprise (INT) Pty Ltd.
29 Grange Road, Cheltenham, VIC 3192, Australia

www.moosetoys.com
info@moosetoys.com

It was Halloween in Shopville!

The Shoppies were excited to celebrate in spooktacular style. But they weren't sure what to do for fun.

"Maybe we should go trick-or-treating!" said Donatina.

"Oooo!" said Jessicake. "Trick-or-treating sounds like a sweet idea!"

"That's too much effort," said Bubbleisha, popping a big bubble lazily.

Donatina thought hard. "Okay, how about we carve jack-o'-lanterns?" she said.

"Too messy!" said Bubbleisha.

Then Rainbow Kate jumped up. "I know! How about we have a costume contest?" she said.

"Yes!" said Popette. "I love that idea.
I can't wait to walk down our costume runway!"

Everyone cheered. Even Bubbleisha looked happy.
Nothing was more fun than dressing up!

However, Peppa-Mint didn't cheer as loudly as her friends. Instead, she looked worried.

All the Shoppies ran back to their homes to get ready for the contest. But Peppa-Mint walked home slowly. Lippy Lips ran up to her.

Lippy Lips asked,
"Is anything wrong?
You don't look happy."

"Well . . .
I don't know
what to wear," said
Peppa-Mint.

Lippy Lips wanted to help Peppa-Mint. "Maybe you could dress up like a witch?" suggested Lippy.

Just then, the friends saw Popette prancing down the sidewalk and wearing a witch's hat.

"Okay, not a witch," said Lippy Lips. "Maybe a vampire!" Before Peppa-Mint could answer, Cocolette swooped by, wearing a vampire cloak and fangs.

Peppa-Mint sighed. "Oh, no!" she cried. "Everyone is taking all the good costumes. Now I really don't know what to wear!"

Lippy Lips tried to cheer up Peppa-Mint. "It'll be okay! All you need is something that no one else has. I bet you can make something special!" Lippy said encouragingly.

Peppa-Mint was excited. "You're right!
I bet I can make something! Thanks, Lippy!"
And off Peppa-Mint ran to get ready.

But Peppa-Mint discovered that making a costume wasn't easy. She glued fancy headdresses together, and they fell apart.

She tried to be a pretty butterfly, but her wings broke.

She tried making a pumpkin costume, but it was too heavy to wear.

"Oh, no!" Peppa-Mint wailed. "I'm never going to finish making a costume!"

Just then, Bubbleisha dropped by. "Come on, Peppa-Mint," Bubbleisha said. "We don't want to be late to the party."

Peppa-Mint sighed. "I think you're just going to have to go without me," she said.

"I don't think so!" Bubbleisha said. "I know just what you should wear. I'll help you make your costume!"

Later, all the BBFs were at Jessicake's house in their spooky costumes. Everyone had really dressed up!

Popette was so excited that she couldn't stop showing off her outfit. "I'm a pretty witch!" she cried.

"And I can be your cat!" said Peppa-Mint.

Bubbleisha had drawn a little nose and whiskers on Peppa-Mint's face, and then the friends had made a headband with kitty ears! Now, Peppa-Mint was the cutest, spookiest kitty ever!

"Oh! You look so cute!" said Popette.

Jessicake said, "Everyone looks too cute to choose just one winner! So, let's just have the best Halloween party instead."

"That sounds purr-fect," said Peppa-Mint. "Happy Halloween!"